ALL TOGETHER NOW

Story based on episode written by Kim Thompson.
www.doodlebops.com

© Disney

COOKIE JAR™

COOKIE JAR™

D1313640

DOODLEBOPS™ and COOKIE JAR™ & © 2007 Cookie Jar Entertainment, Inc.
Used under license by Carson-Dellosa Publishing Co., Inc.

ISBN 978-1-60095-247-0

"You've got a show today, and you've got to play," Jazz reminded the band. "So, no more shirking; let's get working."
"We will!" the Doodlebops promised as she left.

"I've got a new song, too!" said Moe. "Want to hear it?" He hopped over to his drums and started to play. Rooney and Deedee winced.

Deedee just shook her head. Deedee looked sternly at Rooney and Moe. "I'm going to practice my new song with or without you," she said.

"Go right ahead," Rooney answered. "I'm going to practice my song."

Meanwhile, Moe was banging away on his drums. He played so loudly that Mr. Moosehead's antlers fell off!

"So," Bob asked, smiling, "are you ready for your concert today?"
"My song is ready," Deedee told him.

The bus pulled up in front of the concert hall. The Doodles waved to their fans and ran to the backstage door.

Deedee sighed. "It's true. We're going to have to figure this one out by ourselves."

Jazz was waiting for them backstage. "You're on right away. What song will you play?" she asked.

The three Doodlebops looked at each other unhappily. "We can't decide," Deedee told her.

"Jazz can decide for us," said Rooney.

"Listen to my song, Jazz!" yelled Moe. He pulled up a stool and starting drumming on it with his drumsticks.

"Now, listen to mine!" said Deedee. She started playing at the same time.

Rooney's eyes widened. "Hey, that's not bad!" He started playing his song on his guitar. All three of the songs fit together. It was perfect. Nothing was missing now.

"Our songs all go together!" cried Moe.
Deedee laughed. "We should have been playing together all along," she said.

Rooney nodded. "Like a team . . . like a band," he said.